THE LITTLE COMPANION

THE LITTLE COMPANION

CHAS LEONARD

Library of Congress Control Number:		2021902949
ISBN:	Hardcover	978-1-6641-1479-1
	Softcover	978-1-6641-1477-7
	eBook	978-1-6641-1478-4

Print information available on the last page.

Rev. date: 02/19/2021

To order additional copies of this book, contact:
Xlibris
UK TFN: 0800 0148620 (Toll Free inside the UK)
UK Local: 02036 956328 (+44 20 3695 6328 from outside the UK)
www.Xlibrispublishing.co.uk
Orders@Xlibrispublishing.co.uk
826221

CONTENTS

I got to do the job I was given to do. I want it completed in a practical way of work.

That's my mindset; I would want to do the job I was given to do.

Now how about Revenge?

I must remember that writing all I have is my revents and revenge.

A word here then: hold your beliefs lightly to you and hold the light to you, for then the light will be with you.

I have started to be happy with the way I look, my weight, and also the way I am.

An old woman told me once that metal will turn on us and then the world itself. Maybe the same thing with wood and plastic will happen to us all.

The Liveveird Servant is no longer. A servant of the service maybe.

Klee—Paul.

Everything comes from something.

Everything comes from a dot, and everything goes back into that dot.

Infinity = 2 because it is you and I.

People don't give themselves enough time to wait until they feel better and to have forgiven people for their very silly behaviour to them.

To expect loss and hurt and to forgive the pain of our suffering and move on, not taking the pain on to other people, is our success story.

Mental Health Illness takes a long time to diagnose and treat accordingly because it is different for each one of us. It develops throughout the course of our lives, sometimes hugely.

Taking pills is a process which can take years to come to terms with and come to a positive outcome for the patient and the patient's family.

The secret glint you have for a person you have created a baby with will always be there. You will always have it, man and woman, separated, divorced, or not. It's in the eyes and only in the eyes, and we should not.

No one owns another person; you don't own each other.

It's just the same old thing, the craziness of the world now and then. It is the love of it then.

I remember becoming ill. I thought a lone motorcyclist going down and around the street where we lived was a hired assassin out to kill me. I ran out of the house and all about the area and took off some of my clothes because I thought they contained a tracking device. The police picked me up and asked a few questions, gave me a drink of water, and put me in a cell until my parents arrived.

This was my first episode. I was twenty-six years old and studying Architecture. I kept on cracking up at the critiques when everyone else took them just as the normal thing, although they also recognised them as slightly unpleasant.

When I was back at home, I was visited by a doctor, who gave me some tablets, but they were too strong and made my jaw clamp very uncomfortably.

I remember being frightened of a book I had bought, thinking that it had contained secret information and that it was bugged, so I went and hid it in the local woods, hiding from my parents as if I were in a war as shown on television.

I later ran back to the woods and recovered the book several days later. It seems strange to me that I remembered exactly where it was, wrapped up in cling film.

From there it was to the hospital for my first psychiatric stay. I refused to eat at first because of concerns that the food was poisonous. Then my parents brought some dinner on a tray, and I began eating again.

It was a slow start to taking medication, and it was several years at the 2000 millennium before I decided to take the responsibility of taking my medication properly.

Time has moved on now to 2018, and I just take one day at a time, not knowing what we face in the future because I do not know.

Last weekend, I got very drunk while on a short break visiting friends, and it has taken a full week to get over it. I keep on taking cigarettes and then stopping them again, and I worry about the Narcissism of living life for the future instead of just each day as it comes.

Here are a few favourite recipes:

Mozzarella and fresh tomatoes with salt and pepper and sunflower oil.

Cottage pie made with beef and onion using Worcestershire sauce, a vegetable stock cube, Italian herbs, and a bay leaf.

Fine green beans with brie warmed through.

Fish pie made with cheese sauce after cooking the fish in the milk.

Fried salmon with spring onions and chilies with broccoli and cheese.

Our special nights out are getting a pizza from the local restaurant and eating it at home.

1984

There was also a young man intent on internally robbing a bank from the inside whilst, outside, another computer on the job! Instead he was walking on the streets in the summer heat. Quite sweaty actually.

I can remember our meeting in a Royal outlet where I don't have a clue what was going on.

Again in the heat of summer! I think some bank manager was running short of money, or had potentially all these accounts of robbery ended up in the same place?

Also not forgetting the Barclays Cash Machines Robbery, which apparently got stopped mid-flow with an accusation of intention.

In the 1980s and through financial miscalculations, we could all be lamenting over them for evermore and for too much!

There was a bank robbery—someone had put their cup of tea as a formal bank document and was too scared to show it at the next meeting in case it made them look as haphazard as they obviously were!

Oh well, we're all humans and have our sloppily moments. Blaming it on to an innocent customer makes for somewhat of a macabre incident.

'What a darkened mindset', I hear some people say of the innocent customer.

Sometimes I conclude that we are all just in the wrong place at the wrong time and get a clobbering! Unlucky and lucky, we all get it.

There was also a trip to an internal/external computer office to take the heat off Mr Smith. Oh well, unlucky trip there then. Epson/Canon was guilty! Poor Symantec, they didn't deserve it, did they?

MY TWO SILVER SALVERS

Keith and Terry

Terry and Keith saved my sanity by lying to me for the last few years of my life in Strood. Keith's place was a melody of broken items and untidiness, and Terry lived with his mummy in a tidy two-up two-down.

We were all a band of Merrymen who escaped the realisms of life by laughing and crying to one another. A human was founded on whom of each of there I liked the best. That game never ended. Their wealth was shown in cups of tea and burgers and chips at the local Milano's and teas and coffees at The Crumbs.

We all walked a lot around town. There were others in their group, a cyclist, a gardener, and a gold saver called Alan.

I still talk Wiltshire in my ooohs and ahhs and yeahs.

I know their friendship, and it extended to my husband when they saw him at my flat in Cashes Green. Without these two, I wouldn't be here today.

It's man that saves the world, and they do it through the word.

Steady, containable, and full of fast fun, they rocked my world.

Thank you to all of You.

To hold our beliefs light.

FREEDOM TO VIEW

Seeing ourselves

We must be allowed to view freely.

When we admire without feeling guilty about it, then we are freed from guilty thoughts that lead to irritation.

Anger results from irritation and will hide itself until it bursts from us.

In undetermined ways, we are being told not to see to ourselves.

In every person, there is a dominant personality and a recessive one, and in some people, these swap over from time to time.

Anger makes us do what we would not ever be happy of ourselves either in violent or surreptitious ways. We must be allowed to see freely and let our feelings go away.

SPROGS

There I was in Foston, NR Grantham, lincs, and there was a situation going on in the 1970s.

I was eleven and leggie just starting to look pretty.

There was a sad old single woman teacher who was known to be sexually misfuncted.

I passed by her house one day, and I could hear that I was being cursed. She had two copper beach trees in the garden.

There was an intruder after that.

Many SPROGS later—and I dearly loved them all—I married and have been happy!

People were chastened in the 1970s, and trouble happened because of it. There was a man in the RAF who was also chastened for the way he was.

The man chastened me.

I have sprogs who passed away and SPROGS who are still alive today, and needless to say, I know nothing of them.

I am learning to release them from my mind and to move on in my brain.

For today is today, and tomorrow never comes.

FRENCH ANGLAISE!

Retirements?

To pense que Sierra est Romeo? Marseilles!

Pour ouvrez le truc elles est necessaire an se trouve le clef.

El marquise sout Daccords's.

El nom es St. Peter's.

El mar es le truncke.

Okay? We don't know which way France we'll go if we go to war with Russia due to their large Arabic population.

Les scales on se sur cest 'es malovelent de se ces't sure.

J'espere we all die happy!

To Promote Harmonious Relationships.

REMEMBRANCE

PAIN ANGUISH'S SOMETHING
It's just honest trust.

The work experience of a fifteen-year-old doing the Silver Duke of Edinburgh's Award took over my emotional maturity, and I broke down and cried.

I was overcome when working in an old retirement home.

The sadness of bedsores and cries of Alzheimer's sufferers overwhelmed me. The people I was working for had suffered in WWI and WWII, and now they were again in Hardship and Pain.

The wars are dementing everyone for a good cause and a good end, namely to procure a way to a continuing of the world. It is always a success and always for good and the endeavours rewarded in remembrance. We have always moved as a civilisation, and we will make sure we always do.

The Disparities of Life

Moral Integrity

Some like smart poor.

Some like smart rich.

Some have lost family love and money, so they draw one another apart and let themselves go on and die into a new life whatever it may mean.

Some seek for reassurance in what they have achieved; some others abhor it and will not stand for it.

At the end of the day, we all want to be the best to ourselves, and from that, a smaller self appeals.

We are bing people, all of us, and some in this world are small, and some are larger.

Please don't make us feel we have to be physically smaller to save money whether it be in the NHS or our own personal monies.

Lying we all do at some stage of life, whether it be younger or older or just slap being in the middle.

Description: It's for gossip and suing.

SUPERMAN AND LOIS LANE ARE GOD'S parents, and Superman's parents came from the universe where they returned to, to be with their parents again as their parents were getting elderly, and they needed their children to help them again.

God had a son called Jesus, and he was born out of Mary by an incarnation of the holy spirit, and his earth father was called Joseph.

God also made some people out of rib and some people out of sand because he was god. He wanted to repopulate the world. So we are all halfies.

So we are looked over and taken care of by the universe, but we all have our own free will which we are expected to take control over and to lead the best possible lives we can with it by being as good as it is possible to be good in our lives then. So we are all half god and half human then.

We're all halfies. Half God and Half Human. REINCARNATION.

So we are in resurrection then. Yes, we are.

LUC

A Mental Depression

Luc opened out his arms and sank into the cold drizzle of the rain at six thirty in the morning. He had woken up and been stung by his dreams and a feeling that he could only describe as being Down.

Kissing the air, he breathed in deeply and slowly counted to three and then exhaled fast.

His girlfriend had left him after his daughter turned three years of age, and he was on the route back to insanity or forwards to insanity, whichever way he looked at it.

Theirs had been one row after another on how to talk to their daughter, Elizabeth. Luc thought highly of his daughter, and to him, she was the very princess that was and could say anything if it came to her to say it.

He thought, as he stood there naked on the front of a cliff face, that it was on to God to decide his fate and took a step towards the abyss in his open mind.

Tears poured from his feelings of one relationship let-down to another, remembering his mother who had loved him unconditionally but had been unable to stand up to his father who was a bully to his son, Luc.

Luc thought to go back to his routine of showering hot and cold, but on trying it again, he could not carry it on any further. Perhaps, he thought, he had got too soft and this time thought of his dearly beloved mother who was always making up to him after his father's remissions.

Luc decided to drink and smoke instead. Not much liking the taste of beer, he took to whiskey and soda, knowing there would be debts to pay for this as he did only have very little money.

He had read about pan and learned about the lyre and the sweetest sound of lies that are always readily believed. Greek and Roman Myths explained us all, so he thought.

Alcoholism came swiftly, and he did not attend the meetings with his daughter, preferring the lamenting of a lost life.

Going back to his old family home was tormenting, but this time, he painted it in orange-and-sky blue, enamelling the windows and turning it, in his mind, into his very own fishing boat for the catch of the sea.

Walking on his garden naturist temperament, he waved once again at the birds, planes, and helicopters in the sky and whistled softly to drum out the pain in any form of release for him.

At the local pub, he began talking to one or two older men who had known him as a young lad and wanting to include him in their lamenting too.

Fred was a good man who had lost his boat in a hurricane, the only one to survive in a wetsuit.

Fred had the beginnings of Parkinson's, and Luc began to realise a certain kindness in himself once again, then realising that everyone had their problems.

Friendship ensued, and one day, Luc realised that he needed to take his medication again as he was on the way to a counselling meeting due to his wife's insistence.

He had realised that he had become somewhat like his father as his daughter was growing up and too strict on his wife's movements.

Luc had a long way to go, but realising now that life is what you make of it even through the stormiest skies, he had to realise that it was the very bottom of the pit and after that came the only way, which was up again to the crest of the wave and feeling a coping level again.

His psychologist helped his mood, and Luc gradually decided to pick up once again then.

JOHN AND RUTH

Church Love

The Devil is a Woman, and God is a Man.

One day, there was a boy called, John and he realised that he knew nothing of some big book called The Bible. He had a thing called Faith but nothing but badness to attach it too.

He had robbed the odd shop and fallen for both boys and girls in frights and, since his early childhood, knew nothing about being honest because he was told that honesty got you nowhere.

He decided to creep into the ugliest building in the town called The Sainte Apostles Church to see if he could take a look at a Bible to decide what he thought of these Heatheners people!

On entering this place, he was surprised to find a piano and made a few tinkles on it! There was a strangest-looking piece of stone like a turret on a castle, and he went around the crooked steps up into it and found a large book! He liked it! And became good straight away! He had found love. John found his true love through the church, although it is sometimes wrong and right and not always for you! When he turned fifteen, he started being a Bible Reader.

That was what Ruth knew anyway—she didn't do anything wrong. She looked up into his deep-blue eyes and vowed to love for evermore.

John knew that it was a darker sexuality he found in The Church, and he knew it was because The Devil walks hand in hand with God. He knew that it would not affect his higher power if he came to an untimely end. Death and Sex Indeed it was because of the darker sexual fantasy.

'Swearing incites the Devil,' said Ruth to John one day, but he explained to Ruth that it was a way of finding out where The Devil was in your life and where the devil was in your life.

'Drunken and Debauched,' said Ruth to John, 'but Christ's blood is alcoholic, so a glass or two to save the day is not bad, is it then!'

THE TOY

Computer Tek

One day, Tek went off on his batteries all day long. His new owner, who was actually a little boy called Tom, didn't mind at all, but his mum and dad went mad.

You see it had triggered a switch in them both. All the little boy could do was to hide him behind a cushion to stifle his noise a bit more then.

The batteries went on remotely, and they had broken the remote controller.

Eventually, they managed to find a house for him out in the garden where he annoyed the neighbours all night.

In the morning, Tek was taken back in the house again where he continued until the dog dismantled his connections.

Poor Tek, it wasn't really his fault.

DESERT RED FOX

Farfair the Camel

There was a camel in Africa, and she was called Farfair.

She plodded along following her mum until one day she was taken to a new home, as far as she was concerned, far, far, and far away.

Her new mum loved her too and made her very warmly welcomed, but she had to follow everything she did, and sometimes it was very hard work indeed.

One day, she went on a caravan trek to an oasis filled with date trees and had carried much on her back.

Tired she was, she settled down to rest for a day and a half. Then they made her walk again, but this time with nothing on her back.

She began to cover her new owner then.

GOD + FOOD

Cat And Dog

There was a cat and a dog. Dog remembered God, and Cat remembered he wanted to be served!

So the home place was very well-guarded until one day Cat died and Dog was morose and forgot that God was there carrying him through his grief.

So Dog got very remorseful and growled at the vicar who came to see him, and then he was put in his kennel to simmer down for a while.

So when he'd had long enough on his own, he started to howl, and so he was let out of his kennel and had his dinner.

Then once his tummy was full again, he remembered God again.

Cat was buried in the garden, and Dog sat faithfully beside the grave time and again.

Love never dies on a good relationship.

HOME LOVE

Of A Gardener

Muriel was inexperienced as a Gardener, so she was uncompromising in her dealings in the Garden.

Compost for everything she thought, but when it ran out, she just put the new plants in anyway.

Mostly Muriel just dug a hole and deposited the plant, taking care to water it before and after planting and fixing the soil right up to the top of the stem which adjoined the roots, and they always came through.

Unfortunately, a stag got in to the garden and ate the tops off the roses, but having faith that spring was not quite there, she left them alone, and they all started to grow back, however, a little stouted for their ordeal.

The olive tree did not survive, however, and was removed.

It's great to have a little pair of dippers, she thought, as she cut away all the weeds from around her plants.

HOSPITAL

Spirits

What a lovely room, Muriel thought as she opened the door to what would be their room for the following four weeks.

Clean, warm, airy, and with a large bathroom. There was a kettle and a few sachets of tea, coffee, milk, and sugar, just right for settling in.

The hospital was a short walk away, and walking a little every day was very good for their treatment.

One week passed quickly, and then on to the next with hope and a glimmer of success.

The breakfast vouchers were an excellent way to finish off the kindness bestowed on them, and the gratitude was warmly felt by both of them.

Receiving treatment is hard and takes strength and courage to complete it; however, time will tell if they had the strength to go through with it all and complete the hospital guidelines to fruition.

IN PAST TIMES

A Day At Home

It's August, and there's been a dreadful storm for two weeks solid.

I'm thinking it is the start of winter, but my husband just laughs and says, 'No, it's just here.'

I arrived in a snowstorm followed by four weeks of gales.

We walked around the harbour every night in snow jackets, and I found it very exhilarating and still do love a good storm.

The smell here is of fish, and apparently we all smell of fish to other areas in the country.

Above all this, Lochinver is a beautiful and picturesque port village and very protective of all its inhabitants whether doing bad or good or nothing.

Eleven years on, I believe I'll stay forever here.

TENNIS ELBOW

You're just like an old Fuffa Fish 'cept you are run mother.

So you've had enough? Then!

She loved him then. Stuck it in to him and cracked the ceramasist pipe, sucked on it so hard she did.

Tennis elbow: In a myriad of Dreams, fucking Hell, you said it was in the cutlery drawer. I'm full.

She didn't see him again. He'd gone out next door, as the doorbell goes.

OVERSIMPLIFIED

INDIE WRITING
PSYCHOLOGY
In Memory of Tom

He said No! And grappled with his mind to hit the liar she was.

Tossed off, he felt better. Stronger a man, stronger always a man, and he knew it.

Now. You'll do as I am the foreman of this mechanical operation, and you will abide by me.

He chucked the belt at the bed, and she recorded into her lizard frame.

Sex, no. Talking to his stories, YES!

And you will believe me when I say I am going to want off five times a week. She smoked it.

The holy ghost of heroin.

I don't know whether you're a sweet nag or a bloody nag, she thought. He better bring back the Neapolitan ice cream.

Western Star docking on our iceberg. He shifted her off the break.

Rig knew what to do in the Captain's Wheelhouse. Smokey loved a good cuddle.

The hobster pot was a good man.

Good are on him for the wellies.

About stout.

Amen.

R. E.

We'll just get another fucking Cork. Ski 'n' do
or Prosecco.

Vegan Omnivores

VEGETABLE CASSEROLE

Mushroom/cream cheese

Pearl Barley

2 cans, 1 with herbs and chopped tomatoes

3 leeks

Chestnut mushrooms

Rapeseed oil

Salt and pepper

6 jelly cubs stock

Half Pearl Barley and add mushrooms and leeks.

Fry in oil for 5 minutes.

Add 5 1/2 cans of water from the empty tomato can.

Add 6 stock cubs.

After boiling 20 to 30 minutes, add the other half of Pearl Barley and cook further for 30 minutes.

Add Mushroom/cream cheese. Stir and let cool.

Add salt and pepper.

Serves 12.

COUSCOUS

Groundsec currents

Ginger, ground

Water

Salt and pepper

Put water and couscous in a pan and heat to hydrate couscous.

Add currents, ginger, salt, and ground chillies.

AUBERGINE FRUIT

Flat-leaf parsley, chopped and dried
Aubergine, dried and chopped
Pasta, dried and chopped
Salt

Rehydrate with water to a paste.

WHEAT FLOUR

Vegetable oil

Orange Flavonoids

Chilli powder

Flower Water/Rose water

Flour

Mix together and bake.

POTATOES

Oranges

Dried, chopped tomatoes

Rosemary, chopped and dried

Potatoes, washed, with skin on

Bake the potatoes.

Make into chews.

PLANTAINS AND VANILLA

Rapeseed oil for cooking plantains
Then mix with vanilla.
PLANTAINS are a sweetheart with a skin.
Cook them in the skin.

MANGOES AND COFFEE

Chopped Mangoes and bitter coffee

Mix together.

Coffee beans have carcinomas is the best
goodness for vitality.

VICTORIA PETITE

They Rose Queen Victoria because she was an Empress. An American Man Using Chloroform performed the addictive trick Half-Handed.

Chlorophyll.

Don't like the word *Rose*, nothing to do with the money. The flight fighting has to do with the word *Rose* associated with Britain's war of the Roses.

Tea it has hung on to now.

The foul language BFAB from the top talkers with Queen Sapphire was sent to warn of a civil war starting with PetiTe Victoria, South Africa.

Empires have to pay.

Civil war in Yemen and the United States means Britain's economy is getting squashed smaller.

Two Eggs in a basket: to understand what we want to understand, to be how we want to be.

Imagine two eggs boiling in a pan and imagine the pan and the eggs as one with the water as you.

WHEY DINNER

Maize Nuggets

Eggplant

Feta

Sausage/sausage meat

Redcurrant Jelly

Cut Aubergine into chips and put in casserole dish with broken feta cheese, sausages/sausage meat, and maize Nuggets and redcurrant Jelly, and shake the casserole. Put in the oven at 150 degrees centigrade for 45 minutes.

Use a metal casserole dish or allow for extra time.

Printed and bound by CPI Group (UK) Ltd, Croydon, CR0 4YY